Out and
About

dick bruna

miffy
at the
zoo

EGMONT

Said Miffy's father one fine day

I have a good idea

I'm going to the zoo today

come with me, Miffy dear.

Going to the zoo, cried Miffy Bun

oh yes, that will be great

but it's a long, long way away

I hope the train's not late.

And so they travelled on the train

the proper big train, too

the train ran very very fast

and Miffy watched the view.

They must have travelled for an hour

but now they're there, you see

and Father Bun steps out and says

come Miffy, follow me.

At first they went along a walk

where cheerful parrots sat

the parrots shouted, hello Miff

for parrots talk like that.

And then – what's that? cried Miffy

that funny little horse

a horse with stripes all over it

a zebra? Yes, of course.

They also saw a kangaroo

in front she had a pouch

and that was for her baby roo

as comfy as a couch.

And next they saw an elephant

he's so huge, Miffy said

and look, he's stretching out his trunk

to take a piece of bread.

And have you seen the monkey there

he's swinging on a tree

with just one hand, but monkeys find

it easy, as you see.

Now the giraffes, oh goodness me

their necks are very long

but they won't hurt you, Miffy dear

no, nothing will go wrong.

And when the day was nearly done

now, Miffy, you decide

perhaps the giant tortoise? Yes!

that was a lovely ride.

So everything was over now

the train was standing near

and in the train Miff fell asleep

sleep well now, Miffy dear.

miffy's library

miffy
miffy's dream
miffy goes to stay
miffy is crying
miffy at the seaside
miffy at school

miffy at the playground
miffy at the zoo
miffy in hospital
miffy in the tent
miffy's bicycle
miffy in the snow

miffy's house
miffy at the gallery
miffy's birthday
miffy goes flying
miffy the fairy

"nijntje in de dierentuin"
First published in Great Britain 1997 by Egmont Books Limited
239 Kensington High Street, London W8 6SA
Publication licensed by Mercis Publishing bv, Amsterdam
Original text Dick Bruna © copyright Mercis Publishing bv, 1963
Illustrations Dick Bruna © copyright Mercis bv, 1963
Original English translation © copyright Patricia Crampton, 1996
The moral right of the author has been asserted.
Printed in Germany by sachsendruck GmbH, Plauen
All rights reserved
ISBN 1-4052-1695-6
10 9 8 7 6 5 4 3 2